BLIMEY!

LIGHTS

adventure

CHEWIE

ALIEN SPACESHIPS

Tag! you're it!

Fire-Breathing Dragon

hope

TO:
FROM:

EXCITING

CaMPiNG

SLEEPING BAG

pretend

OLIVER

POPCORN

CIRCUS TENT

CHOCOLATE

THE MOON'S MADE OF CHEESE... PASS THE PEAS. PRETTY PLEASE...

SING

ISBN: 978-0-9897937-9-7

Manufactured in the United States of America.
Fifth Edition, January 2016.

Publisher: UHCCF/Adventure
Author: Meg Cadts and UHCCF
Illustrator: Samantha Fitch
Contact: UnitedHealthcare Children's Foundation

UnitedHealthcare Children's Foundation
MN017-W400 | PO Box 41
Minneapolis, MN 55440-0041

1-855-MY-UHCCF
1-855-698-4223
UHCCF.org

Oliver & Hope's

ADVENTURE
UNDER THE STARS

Written By Meg Cadts
Illustrated By Samantha Fitch

"Hey, great job, Chewie!" said Oliver.

"We can add that stick to the batch Hope and I found."

Hope's pile wasn't as big as the one her friends made, but she decided it was still pretty good, since she's a butterfly and can't carry very much.

The three friends were just getting ready for their next adventure – camping for the first time.

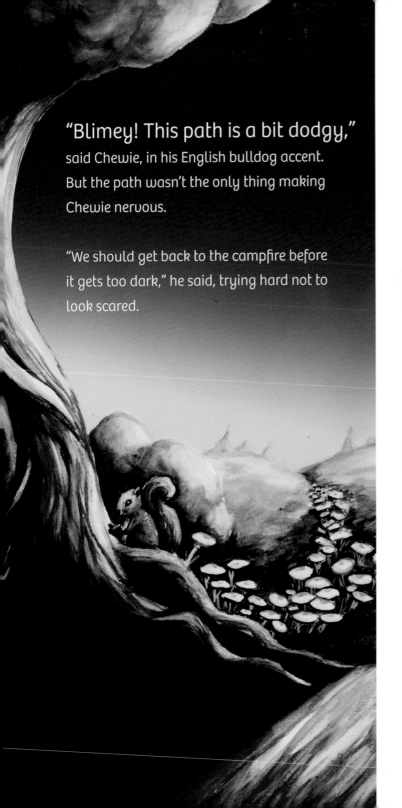

"Blimey! This path is a bit dodgy," said Chewie, in his English bulldog accent. But the path wasn't the only thing making Chewie nervous.

"We should get back to the campfire before it gets too dark," he said, trying hard not to look scared.

As the stars rose above, the moon cast its white glow, creating big shadows that made strange shapes all around.

All the friends used flashlights to find their way. Except for Hope. Partly because she could see pretty well in the dark, but mainly because they don't make butterfly-sized flashlights.

"Your shadow looks like a giant monster," said Oliver. "And yours looks like... well, it looks like a bear, but a much bigger bear," barked Chewie.

Everyone had fun imagining
what the different
shadows looked like.
Then they reached their
campfire and
imagined something
TRULY AMAZING.

Through the glow of their lights and the stars above,
the friends pretended they saw a fire-breathing dragon...
a **Very HUNgry** fire-breathing dragon.

"I'm not going to let that dragon steal our grub!"

barked Chewie.

Then he quickly grabbed the marshmallows before they were all roasted.
Chewie was having so much fun, he almost forgot he was afraid of the dark.

Of course, the dragon wasn't a dragon at all, but simply the shadow of their friend Millie.
For a small owl, she made a big impression.

The friends told stories, stuffed their bellies and made up silly songs like,

**"THE MOON'S MADE OF CHEESE...
PASS THE PEAS, PRETTY PLEASE."**

The friends admired the stars shining brightly in the sky.
Oliver wondered out loud,

"Are they all the same?"

Hope thought, "They look similar from afar, but the closer you get,
the more unique they become. Just like each of us."
But, she decided to just keep this idea to herself for now.

"Who, who..." Millie said nervously,
"who do you think is coming?"
as she saw some of the lights getting closer.

The friends imagined 10 bright spaceships approaching. Soon they were all running around playing alien tag, which is pretty much like regular tag, except you play it with alien spaceships.

"Tag! You're it!"
hooted Millie.

Of course, the aliens weren't aliens at all. They were fireflies dancing in the night.
But pretending they were from outer space was a lot more fun.

Hope flew up close to one of the fireflies and thought,

"You're the most beautiful thing I've ever seen."

And the firefly thought the same thing about
Hope's colorful wings.

By now it was late and everyone was a little tired from
chasing imaginary dragons and aliens all night.
They grabbed their flashlights and headed into the tent.

"Time to get ready for bed,"
Oliver said with a mouth full of toothpaste.

"Tops & bottoms."

"Side to Side."

By the time Chewie found his flashlight, everyone had disappeared.
Once again, the dark made him feel scared.

"Where are my mates?" he wondered **Nervously**.

As he slowly walked toward the tent

Chewie imagined
a nighttime circus tent!
Filled with elephants, giraffes
and acrobats spinning in the air.
At least that's what it looked like to Chewie,
who stood frozen in amazement.

When Chewie finally arrived, he discovered who the real stars of the circus were. Oliver, Hope and Millie were all laughing and dancing as they used their hands and feet (and wings for some) to make SHadOW PUPPets.

Chewie popped into the tent, flexed his muscles and cheered...

"Introducing the amazing
Chewie the Great!"

Soon the lights dimmed on the circus and the friends tucked
each other into their sleeping bags.

"Who would have thought..." asked Millie,
"that we'd see so many exciting things
in one night camping?"

"And who knew dragons liked
s'mores so much?" laughed Oliver.

Oliver's friends giggled
themselves to sleep.
Including Chewie, who decided
the dark wasn't quite as
scary as it used to be.

High above, the moon and stars cast friendly new shadows to be discovered another night.

UnitedHealthcare
Children's Foundation®

Stories that inspire.
You can help us write the next chapter.

The Oliver & Hope® series tells stories of adventure, curiosity and perseverance. Stories of hope and imagination. And, in many ways, these same elements help guide the mission of the UnitedHealthcare Children's Foundation (UHCCF), a 501(c)(3) charitable organization. UHCCF supports the UnitedHealth Group's mission to "help people live healthier lives" and aligns under the enterprise values of Integrity, Compassion, Relationships, Innovation and Performance.

Each year, UHCCF offers grants to help children gain access to medically-related services that are not covered, or not fully covered, by their parents' commercial health insurance plan. It is through these grants — and the shared commitment of our staff, volunteers, sponsors and recipients — that truly inspiring stories unfold.

The best part is you can be a part of these stories, which continue to write new chapters each year. If you know a family that could benefit from a UHCCF medical grant, you can help make an introduction. And, if you are able to offer your time or resources, we have many ways for you to get involved. Even the smallest contribution can help make a major impact in the lives of the families we work with.

Visit UHCCF.org for more Oliver & Hope® stories and activities, and to learn more about how you can be part of our story.

UHCCF.org | 1-855-MY-UHCCF | 1-855-698-4223

UnitedHealthcare Children's Foundation
MN017-W400 | PO Box 41 | Minneapolis, MN 55440-0041